Here's what kids have to say to
Mary Pope Osborne, author of
the Magic Tree House series:

*Your books are so interesting that I feel like I
am in there.*—K. C.

*I like your Jack and Annie books so much
that I would never throw or give them away.*
—Peter F.

I bet 200,000 people love your stories.
—Esther Mary D.

*Just please keep on making these books for
the rest of your life!*—Taylor C.

Your books are the best in the universe!!!
—Danny Z.

*I wish you'd come out with more than a
thousand, thousand books.*—Dylan H.

Write to Mary Pope Osborne yourself!
See the next page for the address.

Dear Reader,

While I was trying to decide what to do for book number nine, kids kept asking me to send Jack and Annie under the ocean.

"But how will they breathe and talk underwater?" I asked.

After a number of kids suggested a submarine, I began researching the subject and learned about mini-subs, and that settled it.

So, thanks to all the kids who've helped me—and keep helping me. I feel as if we're all having these adventures together—you, me, Jack, and Annie.

Where do we go next? And what do you think will happen when we get there? Let me know....

Mary Pope Osborne

P.S. If you'd like to share *your* Magic Tree House ideas with Mary Pope Osborne, you can write to her at this address:

Mary Pope Osborne
Random House, Inc.
201 East 50th Street
Mail Drop 28-2
New York, NY 10022

MAGIC TREE HOUSE #9

Dolphins at Daybreak

by Mary Pope Osborne

illustrated by Sal Murdocca

A FIRST STEPPING STONE BOOK

Random House 🏠 New York

For Mattie Stepanek

Text copyright © 1997 by Mary Pope Osborne.
Illustrations copyright © 1997 by Sal Murdocca.
All rights reserved under International and Pan-American Copyright
Conventions. Published in the United States by Random House, Inc., New York,
and simultaneously in Canada by Random House of Canada Limited, Toronto.

http://www.randomhouse.com/

Library of Congress Cataloging-in-Publication Data
Osborne, Mary Pope. Dolphins at daybreak / by Mary Pope Osborne ;
illustrated by Sal Murdocca.
    p.   cm. — (Magic tree house series : #9) "A first stepping stone book."
SUMMARY: Their magic tree house takes Jack and Annie deep into the sea, where
they meet up with dolphins, sharks, and octopi as they search for the answer to
an ancient riddle.
ISBN 0-679-88388-X (pbk.) — ISBN 0-679-98338-4 (lib. bdg.)
[1. Marine animals—Fiction. 2. Submarines—Fiction. 3. Riddles—Fiction.
4. Magic—Fiction. 5. Tree houses—Fiction.] I. Murdocca, Sal, ill. II. Title.
III. Series: Osborne, Mary Pope. Magic tree house series : #9.
PZ7.081167Do 1997 [Fic]—dc20 96-30943

Printed in the United States of America   30 29 28 27 26 25

Random House, Inc. New York, Toronto, London, Sydney, Auckland

Contents

1

Master Librarians

Jack stared out the kitchen window.

The sun was not up yet. But the sky was growing lighter.

Jack had been awake for a long time. He had been thinking about the dream he'd had—the dream about Morgan le Fay.

The tree house is back, Morgan had said. *I'm waiting.*

Jack wished that dreams were real. He missed Morgan's magic tree house.

"Jack!" His little sister Annie appeared in the doorway. "We have to go to the woods *now!*" she said.

"Why?" Jack asked.

"I had a dream about Morgan!" exclaimed Annie. "She said the tree house is back and she's waiting for us!"

"That was *my* dream," said Jack.

"Oh, wow," said Annie. "She told you, too? So it *must* be important."

"But dreams aren't real," said Jack.

"Some dreams aren't. But this one is," said Annie. "I can just feel it." She opened the back door. "I'll see you later!"

"Wait—wait. I'm coming!" said Jack.

He raced up the stairs. *Having the same dream must mean* something, he thought.

He grabbed his backpack and threw his

notebook and pencil into it.

Then he ran downstairs.

"We'll be back soon, Mom!" Jack called into the living room.

"Where you going so early?" his dad called.

"Just for a quick walk!" said Jack.

"It rained last night," called his mom. "Don't get your shoes wet."

"We won't!"

Jack slipped out the door. Annie was waiting for him.

"Let's go!" she said.

The sky was pale gray. The air felt freshly washed.

Jack and Annie ran up their quiet street to the Frog Creek woods.

They headed between the trees. Soon they

came to the tallest oak in the woods. There was a wooden house high in the treetop.

"It *is* back!" whispered Jack.

Someone looked out the window of the tree house—a lovely old woman with long white hair. Morgan le Fay.

"Come up," called the magical librarian.

Jack and Annie climbed up the rope ladder and into the tree house.

In the dawn light, they stared at Morgan le Fay. She looked beautiful in a red velvet robe.

Jack pushed his glasses into place. He couldn't stop smiling.

"We both had dreams about you!" said Annie.

"I know," said Morgan.

"You do?"

"Yes, I sent them to you," said Morgan, "because I need your help."

"What kind of help?" said Jack.

"Merlin the Magician has been up to his tricks again," said Morgan. "So I haven't had any time to collect books for Camelot's library."

"Can we collect them for you?" asked Annie.

"Yes, but in order to gather books through time you must be Master Librarians," said Morgan.

"Oh, well," Annie said sadly.

"But you can *become* Master Librarians," said Morgan, "if you pass the test."

"Really?" said Annie.

"What kind of test?" Jack asked.

"You must show that you know how to do

research," said Morgan, "and show that you can find answers to hard questions."

"How?" said Annie.

"By solving four riddles," said Morgan. She reached into the folds of her robe and pulled out a rolled-up paper.

"The first riddle is written on this ancient scroll," she said. "This book will help you find the answer."

She held out a book. On the cover were the words *Ocean Guide*.

"This is where you have to go," said Morgan.

"The ocean! Oh, boy!" said Annie. She pointed at the cover. "I wish we—"

"Stop!" Jack grabbed Annie's hand. "How will we know if we've found the right answer to the riddle?" he asked Morgan.

"You will know," Morgan said mysteriously. "I promise you will know."

Jack let go of Annie's hand. She pointed again at the cover and finished her wish: "I wish we could go there."

The wind started to blow.

"Are you coming with us, Morgan?" Jack said.

Before Morgan could answer, the tree house started to spin.

Jack squeezed his eyes shut.

The tree house spun faster and faster.

Then everything was still.

Absolutely still.

Jack opened his eyes.

Morgan le Fay was gone.

Only the ancient scroll and the ocean book were left in her place.

2

The Reef

A breeze blew through the window. Sea gulls cried. Waves lapped the shore.

Annie picked up the riddle scroll. She unrolled it. Together she and Jack read the riddle:

> Rough and gray as rock,
> I'm plain as plain can be.
> But hidden deep inside
> There's great beauty in me.
> What am I?

"Let's go find the answer," said Annie.

She and Jack looked out the window. The tree house wasn't in a tree. It was on the ground.

"Why is the ground pink?" said Jack.

"I don't know," said Annie. "But I'm going out there."

"I'm going to do a little research first," said Jack.

Annie climbed out of the tree house.

Jack picked up the ocean book and flipped through it.

He found a picture of a pink island surrounded by water. He read:

This is a coral reef. Corals are tiny sea animals. After they die, their skeletons remain. Over time, the reef builds up from stacks of coral skeletons.

"Oh, man, tiny skeletons," said Jack. He pulled out his notebook and wrote:

Millions of Coral Skeletons

"Jack! Jack! Come look at *this*," cried Annie.

"What is it?"

"I don't know. But you'll love it!" she said.

Jack threw his notebook and the ocean book into his pack. He climbed out the window.

"Is it the answer to the riddle?" he called.

"I don't think so. It doesn't look very plain," said Annie.

She was standing at the edge of the water. Beside her was a strange-looking machine.

Jack hurried over the bumpy coral to get a better look.

The machine was half on the reef and half in the clear blue water. It looked like a huge white bubble with a big window.

"Is it a special kind of boat?" asked Annie.

Jack found a picture of the machine in the ocean book. He read:

> Scientists who study the ocean are called oceanographers. Sometimes they travel in small diving vessels called submersibles, or "mini-subs," to study the ocean floor.

"It's a mini-sub," said Jack. He pulled out his notebook.

"Let's get inside it," said Annie.

"No!" said Jack. Actually, he did want to see what the sub looked like inside. But he shook his head. "We can't. It's not ours."

"Just a teeny peek," said Annie. "It might

14

help us figure out the riddle."

Jack sighed. "Okay. But we have to be careful. Don't touch anything," he said.

"Don't worry," said Annie.

"And take off your shoes so they won't get wet," said Jack.

He and Annie slipped off their shoes and socks and threw them toward the tree house.

Then they stepped carefully over the sharp coral.

Annie turned the handle on the hatch of the mini-sub. It opened.

She and Jack climbed inside. The hatch slammed shut.

The mini-sub was tiny. Two seats faced the big window. In front of the seats was a computer built into a control panel.

Annie sat down.

15

Jack opened the ocean book and read more on the mini-sub page:

> Mini-subs have strong hulls to keep air in and protect those aboard from water pressure. Computers are used to guide the mini-sub through the ocean.

"Oops," said Annie.

"What's wrong?" Jack looked up.

Annie was waving her hands in front of the computer. Now the screen showed a map.

"What's going on?" said Jack.

"I just pressed a few keys—" said Annie.

"What? I said not to touch anything!" said Jack.

An air blower came on. The mini-sub jerked backward.

"Get out!" said Jack.

17

He and Annie scrambled for the hatch.
Jack grabbed the handle.

But they were too late.

The mini-sub slid off the reef.
Then it dove silently down into the deep.

3

Mini-Sub

"You've really done it now, Annie!" said Jack.

"Sorry, sorry. But look out the window!" Annie said. "Look!"

"Forget it! We have to figure this out!" Jack stared at the computer. He saw a row of pictures at the top of the screen.

"What did you do?" he asked.

"I just pressed the ON button," said Annie.

"The screen lit up. And I pressed the starfish."

"That must be the command to go under the water," said Jack.

"Yeah. Then the map came on," said Annie.

"Okay, okay. The map shows the reef," said Jack. "Look! There's the mini-sub on the map! It's moving away from the reef."

"It's like a video game," said Annie. "I bet I know what to do."

Annie pressed a key with an arrow pointing right. The mini-sub on the screen moved right. The real mini-sub turned to the right, also.

"Great!" said Jack with relief. "You press the arrows to steer the mini-sub. So now we can go back."

"Oh, no, not right away," said Annie. "It's so beautiful down here."

"We have to get back to the reef," said Jack. His eyes were still glued to the computer screen. "What if the owners find it gone?"

"Look out the window," said Annie. "Just for one teeny second."

Jack sighed. He pushed his glasses into place and looked up. "Oh, man," he said softly.

Outside the glass was a strange world of bright moving color.

It looked like another planet.

The mini-sub was moving past red, yellow, and blue coral—past little coral mountains, valleys, and caves—past fishes of every color and size.

"Can't we stay a little while? The answer to Morgan's riddle must be here," said Annie.

Jack nodded slowly. She might be right, he thought. Besides, when would they ever get to visit a place like this again?

4

Fish City

There were fish everywhere: floating over the swaying sea grass, eating on the white sandy bottom, peeping out of coral caves.

Some kinds of coral looked like blue fingers or lacy fans. Others looked like deer antlers or lettuce leaves or mushrooms or trees.

Jack read in the book:

> Coral reefs are only found in warm, tropical waters. Nearly 5,000 different

species of fish live around coral reefs
in the Indian and Pacific Oceans.

Jack pulled out his pencil and notebook.
He started to write a list.

<u>Coral Reef Research</u>

warm water
over 5,000 kinds of fish

"Look!" said Annie.

The sub floated past a huge starfish. Then
a pink jellyfish. Then a blue sea horse.

Jack added to his list:

starfish
jellyfish
sea horses

"What is *that?*" said Annie.

Jack saw a creature that looked like a

giant pancake with a long tail.

"A *stingray!*" said Jack. He put that on his list as well.

"And that?" said Annie.

She pointed at the biggest shell Jack had ever seen. It was as big as a footstool.

"I'll have to check on that one," said Jack. He turned the pages of the ocean book. When he got to the page about clams, he read aloud:

> The giant clam of the coral reef is three feet wide and weighs up to 200 pounds.

"Wow," said Annie.

"No kidding," said Jack. He added "giant clam" to his list.

"Dolphins!" cried Annie.

Jack looked up. Two dolphins were peering in the window. They tapped their noses against the glass.

Their eyes were bright. They seemed to be smiling.

Jack laughed. "It's like *we're* in a fish tank—and they're looking at *us*," he said.

"Their names are Sukie and Sam," said Annie. "Sister and brother."

"You're nuts," said Jack.

"Here's a kiss for you, Sukie," Annie said. She pressed her lips to the glass as if she were kissing the dolphin's nose.

"Oh, brother," said Jack.

But the dolphin opened her mouth and tossed her head. She seemed to be laughing.

"Hey, I know the answer to the riddle— dolphins!" said Annie. "They're gray and plain. But they have great beauty inside."

"You forgot the 'rough as a rock' part," said Jack. "Dolphin skin looks smooth and slippery."

"Oh, right," said Annie.

The dolphins flipped their tails. They swam off into the light blue water.

"Wait! Don't go!" called Annie. "Sukie!"

But the dolphins were gone.

"It's time for us to go, too," said Jack. He was afraid someone might be looking for the mini-sub.

"But we haven't solved the riddle," said Annie.

Jack studied the bright underwater world.

"I don't see the answer," he said. "There's nothing plain at all out there."

"Then maybe the answer's in the mini-sub," said Annie.

They looked around the tiny space.

"I'll check the computer," said Jack. He studied the row of pictures at the top of the screen.

He pressed the book picture.

The words SHIP'S LOG flashed onto the screen.

5

Two Eyes

"What's a ship's log?" said Annie.

"It's a diary of an ocean trip," said Jack.

He peered at the computer screen and read a log entry:

MONDAY, JULY 5

"Hey, that was just last week," said Jack. He read further:

COLLECTED ROCK AND SHELL SAMPLES

MAPPED OCEAN FLOOR

FOUND TINY CRACK IN HULL

"This is like your notebook," said Annie.

"Yeah, the oceanographer was writing notes on the computer," said Jack.

Jack and Annie read further:

TUESDAY, JULY 6

CRACK HAS WIDENED

MUST RETURN TO REEF SOON

"A crack where?" said Annie.

"I don't know," said Jack. He read further:

WEDNESDAY, JULY 7

MORE TINY CRACKS

CANNOT BE FIXED

HEADING BACK TO REEF TODAY

"Uh-oh. This doesn't sound good," said Jack. He read further:

THURSDAY, JULY 8

DEFECTIVE SUB

RETURN TO REEF

LEAVE FOR HELICOPTER TO TRANSPORT

TO JUNKYARD

"'Defective' means broken, right?" said Annie.

"Yep," said Jack.

"So this sub is broken, right?" said Annie.

"Yep," said Jack. "And it was waiting to be taken away by a helicopter. To a junkyard."

"Yikes," said Annie.

"Now we *really* have to get back," said Jack.

"Let's try pressing the waves picture," said Annie.

She pressed the waves picture on the computer screen.

The mini-sub began to rise slowly.

"Oh, good," said Jack.

The sub went past a small coral mountain. It went past schools of fish and waving plants.

"Oh!" gasped Annie.

Jack gasped, too.

Two eyes were staring out from behind a giant sea plant. They looked human—except they were as big as golf balls.

The sub moved past the giant plant. Jack breathed a sigh of relief.

"What—? Whose—?" sputtered Annie.

"Don't ask," said Jack.

They stared back at the plant.

Just then, a long arm came out from behind it.

Then another arm came out.

Then another—and another—and another—and another—and another—and another!

Jack and Annie stared in horror at a giant octopus.

"It's coming after us," said Annie.

Slowly, the octopus crept through the water. Its eight arms reached for the mini-sub.

6

C-R-A-C-K

The octopus hugged the mini-sub. Each of its eight arms had two rows of suckers. The suckers stuck to the window.

The mini-sub stopped.

The octopus stared at Jack and Annie with huge, human-like eyes.

"I don't think it wants to hurt us," whispered Annie. "It's just curious."

"I—I'm going to research it," said Jack.

His hands shook as he flipped through the

pages of the ocean book.

He found a picture of an octopus and read aloud:

> The octopus tends to be a gentle, shy creature. Sometimes, though, curiosity gets the best of it and it comes out of hiding.

"Aw. See, I told you, he's shy," said Annie. She yelled to the octopus, "Hi! I'm Annie! He's Jack!"

"Oh, brother," moaned Jack. He read further:

> But the octopus has huge strength. Each of its arms, or tentacles, has many suckers, which act like rubber suction cups. It is nearly impossible to free an object from their grasp.

"Oh, great," said Jack. "We'll never get rid of this thing."

Just then, Jack felt a drop hit his arm. Water. He looked up at the ceiling.

"Uh-oh," said Annie.

A thin crack ran along the ceiling. Smaller cracks branched out from it.

Water dripped from the cracks.

"We found the cracks," said Annie.

"The octopus better let go! Before the whole ceiling breaks!" said Jack.

"Let go, *please*. Please!" Annie shouted at the octopus.

The creature blinked, as if trying to understand her.

"Please! Please! Please!" she shouted.

"Come on, Annie," said Jack. "It doesn't care if you're polite."

The octopus blinked at Jack.

"Get out of here!" Jack yelled at it. "Now! Beat it! Scram! Go!"

The octopus shot a cloud of black liquid into the water and disappeared into the dark cloud. Its long tentacles trailed through the water.

The mini-sub started to rise slowly again.

"You hurt his feelings," Annie said.

"I don't think so…" Something bothered Jack.

He looked back at the ocean book. He read to himself:

> **The octopus squirts black ink to escape its enemies. One of its main enemies is the shark.**

"Oh, no," said Jack.

"What's wrong?" asked Annie.

Jack looked out the window. The water was growing clear again.

A shadowy figure moved toward the mini-sub.

"What is that?" whispered Annie.

The fish was way bigger than the dolphins. And it had a *very* weird head.

Jack could feel his heart nearly stop.

"A hammerhead shark," he breathed. "We're *really* in trouble now."

7

Remain Calm

The shark swam behind the coral.

"Where did it go?" said Annie, peering out the window.

"It doesn't matter," said Jack. "*We* have to get to the top."

"More water's coming in," said Annie.

"Yeah, I know. Come on . . . come on . . . faster!" Jack ordered the mini-sub.

"Even *more* water's coming in," said Annie, "lots more!"

Jack looked up. The water wasn't dripping now—it was spurting.

"A few seconds, a few seconds," said Jack.

Suddenly, the mini-sub burst out of the water. It bobbed on the waves like a cork. The ocean sparkled all around it.

"Safe!" shouted Annie.

Jack felt the water rising around his bare feet.

"Uh—not really . . . " he said.

"Oops," said Annie. "The octopus must have made cracks in the bottom, too."

The water was up to their ankles now.

Jack looked out. He saw the reef in the distance.

"The sub can make it. It doesn't look that far," he said.

"Go, go, *go*," said Annie.

She pressed one of the steering keys.

Suddenly, the screen went blank.

"What's happening?" said Jack.

Annie pressed the key again. Then Jack pressed the other pictures. Nothing happened.

"It's dead," said Annie.

"Oh, great," said Jack.

Now the water was up to their knees.

"I guess we'll have to swim," said Jack. He took a deep breath.

"Right," said Annie. "It's a good thing we had swimming lessons this summer."

"Right," said Jack. "And it's a bad thing we just saw a shark."

Jack quickly found the picture of the shark in the book.

He read aloud:

If you ever see a shark in the water,
don't splash. Swim calmly away.

Jack closed the book.

"We better do the breast stroke," said Annie. "So we won't splash."

"Yep, and stay close," said Jack.

"*Very* close," said Annie. Her eyes were wide. But she seemed very calm.

Jack took a deep breath. He tried to be calm, too. He calmly took off his glasses. He calmly put them and the book into his pack. He calmly put his pack on his back.

Annie opened the hatch.

"Be calm," Annie said. She slipped out of the mini-sub.

"Help," Jack said calmly. He held his nose. Then he calmly lowered himself into the ocean.

8

Swim for Your Life!

Jack moved his arms slowly. He moved his legs slowly. He gently pushed the water out of his way as he did the breast stroke.

Calm, calm, he told himself.

Annie swam beside him. They headed for the reef.

All was calm.

Then Jack saw something out of the corner of his eye.

A dark fin was zigzagging through the water. It was heading toward them.

Jack wanted to splash. He wanted to yell. But he remembered: *calm*.

I better not tell Annie, he thought. *She'll stay calmer if she doesn't know.*

He began to swim faster—then faster. Annie went faster, too.

They both swam as fast, and as calmly, as they could.

Sometimes Annie went even faster than Jack, which made *him* swim faster. And faster.

Jack was so scared that he wasn't tired at all. He was swimming for his life—and for Annie's life, too.

He didn't look back to see if the shark was still there. He didn't want to know.

He just kept his eye on the tree house in the distance. And he kept swimming.

Jack and Annie swam and swam and swam.

It took forever for the tree house to get just a little closer.

Jack realized the reef was farther away than he had thought.

He kept swimming, but his arms and legs felt heavy.

Annie was struggling, too.

"Float!" she said. "Float!"

Jack and Annie turned onto their backs. They floated the way they had learned in swimming class.

We'll just rest for a minute, Jack thought. *Then we'll keep going.*

But the more Jack floated, the more tired he felt. Soon he was too tired even to float. He started to sink.

Then he felt something.

His heart stopped. Something pushed at him in the water.

It was slippery and alive.

Had the hammerhead caught up with them?

Jack shut his eyes and waited for the worst. He waited and waited. Finally, he opened his eyes.

In front of him was a shiny gray head—a dolphin's head!

The dolphin pushed Jack with its nose. It made happy clicking sounds.

"Hooray!" cried Annie.

Jack looked over at her.

She was clinging to the fin of another dolphin! Her dolphin was moving through the water.

Jack grabbed the fin of his dolphin.

Then the two dolphins swam smoothly through the water, pulling Jack and Annie toward the reef.

9

Ouch!

The sun shone on the ocean. It sparkled like a diamond.

Jack felt safe now. His dolphin was taking good care of him.

The dolphins slowed down as they neared the reef.

Jack lowered his feet. He felt the bumpy coral. He let go of the dolphin's fin and stood up in the water.

Annie stood, too.

Then she threw her arms around her dolphin and gave her a big hug.

"Thank you, Sukie!" she cried. And she kissed the dolphin's nose.

Sukie tossed her head and clicked at Annie.

"Kiss Sam now!" Annie said to Jack.

"You're nuts," said Jack.

But Sam nuzzled Jack's head. Then he put his flippers around Jack's neck.

Jack couldn't resist. He threw his arms around the dolphin and gave him a quick kiss.

Sam nodded and made clicking sounds like laughter. Then he turned to Sukie.

The two dolphins chattered to each other for a moment. They nodded at Jack and Annie and swam gracefully away.

"Bye, Sukie! Bye, Sam!" Annie shouted.

"Thanks!" Jack shouted.

The dolphins leapt high into the air. Then they dove back into the water with a SPLASH!

Jack and Annie laughed. "I wish we could swim like that," said Jack.

Jack and Annie watched the dolphins until they disappeared.

"I miss them already," Annie said softly.

"Me too," said Jack.

He sat down in the shallow water.

"I'm really tired," he said.

Annie sat beside him.

"Me too," she said.

The warm water lapped around their shorts and T-shirts.

Jack pulled off his pack. He took out his glasses and put them on. They were blurry with water.

"Guess what," said Annie.

"What?" said Jack.

"I saw the shark when we were swimming," Annie said. "But I didn't tell you. I wanted you to stay calm."

Jack stared at her. "I saw it, too. I just swam faster so you would swim faster."

"And I swam faster so *you* would swim faster," said Annie.

"I guess we swam double-fast then," Jack said. He shook his head with wonder.

"What now?" said Annie.

"We go home," said Jack.

"But we haven't solved Morgan's riddle yet," said Annie.

Jack sighed.

He pulled his notebook out of his pack. It was soaked.

He pulled out the ocean book. It was soaked, too.

"We've failed," he said. "My research is all wet. We'll never be Master Librarians now."

Jack put everything away. "Let's go," he said sadly.

He stood up. Then he started across the pink reef toward the tree house. Annie followed him.

"Ouch!" Annie said.

"What's wrong?" Jack looked back.

"I stepped on something." Annie bent down to rub her foot.

"What?" said Jack. "A shell?"

"Yeah, this . . ." She picked up a large gray shell. "Boy, is it rough. Rough and gray as a rock—"

"*And plain as plain can be!*" whispered

Jack. They had found the answer.

The shell looked like a clamshell—only bigger and with more ridges.

"How could *this* ugly shell be the answer to the riddle?" said Annie. "What about the part that says, 'There's great beauty in me'?"

"Wait—research," said Jack. He opened the soaked ocean book.

The pages were stuck together. But he was able to turn a few.

He found a picture of the gray shell. He read:

> Divers search for oysters in deep
> water. But sometimes oysters wash
> up on reefs or beaches. Inside some
> oysters you can find a pearl. The pearl's
> natural beauty makes it a treasure.

"It must have a pearl inside it!" said Jack.

Annie peered into the crack between the two halves of the shell. "I can't see anything," she said. "How does a pearl get in there, anyway?"

Jack read aloud from the wet page:

> Sometimes a grain of sand will get between the oyster's shell and its skin. This irritates the oyster. So it makes a pearly material to surround the grain of sand. In this way, over a few years, a pearl is formed.

"I can't tell if there's a pearl in there or not," said Annie.

"Maybe we should bang it against a rock," said Jack.

"Now that would *really* irritate the oyster," said Annie.

"Yeah."

"Maybe we should just leave it alone," said Annie.

She gently put the oyster back in the water.

"But how will we know if *oyster* is the right answer to the riddle?" said Jack.

"Morgan said we'll know," said Annie. "Come on."

Jack pushed his glasses into place. Then he and Annie picked up their shoes and socks.

They climbed through the window of the tree house.

Morgan's scroll was lying on the floor.

It was open.

"Look!" said Annie.

She and Jack stared at the scroll. The riddle had faded away.

In its place was one shimmering silver word:

OYSTER

"Morgan's magic," whispered Annie.

Jack let out a huge sigh. "We got it right," he said.

"And here's the Pennsylvania book," said Annie. "Let's go home."

She opened the book. She pointed to a picture of the Frog Creek woods.

"I wish we could go there!" she said.

The wind started to blow.

The tree house started to spin.

The wind blew harder and harder.

Then everything was still.

Absolutely still.

10

The True Pearl

Dawn light slanted into the tree house.

No time at all had passed since they'd left. Day was breaking.

Jack rolled up the ancient scroll. He tucked it into the corner.

"We solved the first riddle," he said. "Three more to go."

"I don't see another scroll," said Annie. "Maybe tomorrow we'll get the next riddle."

"That's okay," said Jack. "I think I need

to rest—and dry out."

His T-shirt and shorts were still soaked. His backpack, too. Only his shoes and socks were dry.

"And this needs to dry out, too," said Annie. She put the wet ocean book in a patch of sunlight.

Then Jack and Annie climbed down the ladder.

They walked through the woods, through leafy shadows and golden light.

They left the woods and started down their street.

"You know, we should have found the answer to the riddle right away," said Jack. "The oyster was on the reef all along."

"I know, but we wouldn't have had so much fun," said Annie.

"Fun?" said Jack. "You call being squeezed by an octopus and chased by a shark *fun?*"

"Don't forget the dolphins," Annie said simply.

Jack smiled. "Right," he said. The dolphins made up for everything. *They* were fun.

"I guess they were the true pearl in the oyster," said Annie.

"Yep…" said Jack. "I wonder what Sam is doing right now."

"Sam?" Annie grinned at him. "You're nuts," she said.

They climbed their steps and went into their house.

"We're back!" Annie shouted.

"Did you get your shoes wet?" their mom called.

"Not one bit," called Jack. Then he and Annie slipped up the stairs to change their clothes.

Don't miss

MAGIC TREE HOUSE #10

GHOST TOWN AT SUNDOWN,

in which Jack and Annie go back in time to the Wild West, where they meet a lonely cowboy and a gang of horse thieves!

Where have you traveled in the Magic Tree House?

Check off the Magic Tree House Books you've read.

❑ **Magic Tree House #1, DINOSAURS BEFORE DARK,** in which Jack and Annie discover the tree house and travel back to the time of dinosaurs.

❑ **Magic Tree House #2, THE KNIGHT AT DAWN,** in which Jack and Annie go to the time of knights and explore a medieval castle with a hidden passage.

Look for these other Random House books
by Mary Pope Osborne!

Magic Tree House books:

Dinosaurs Before Dark (#1)
The Knight at Dawn (#2)
Mummies in the Morning (#3)
Pirates Past Noon (#4)
Night of the Ninjas (#5)
Afternoon on the Amazon (#6)
Sunset of the Sabertooth (#7)
Midnight on the Moon (#8)

Picture books:

Molly and the Prince
Moonhorse

For middle-grade readers:

American Tall Tales
One World, Many Religions
*Spider Kane and the Mystery at
    Jumbo Nightcrawler's*
*Spider Kane and the Mystery Under
    the May-Apple*